A Smokey Lady in Knickers

By

Thorne Smith

Copyright © 2011 Read Books Ltd.
This book is copyright and may not be
reproduced or copied in any way without
the express permission of the publisher in writing

British Library Cataloguing-in-Publication Data
A catalogue record for this book is available from
the British Library

Contents

                                        Page No.

A Biography of Thorne Smith..............1

A Smokey Lady in Knickers..................5

THORNE SMITH

James Thorne Smith Jr. was born at the U.S. Naval Academy in Annapolis, Maryland in 1892. His mother died when he was young, and he spent the early portion of his life in the care of various aunts across the American South. It was during his time in North Carolina that Smith began to tell his first stories and poems, to his cousin and his dog. Smith spent his teens at military academies, where he was an average student who enjoyed his English classes but little else, and eventually graduated in 1910 at the age of eighteen.

After leaving college, Thorne took a job in a New York advertising agency and wrote copy for Dr.

Lyon's Tooth Powder. In 1917, following in the footsteps of his father – a semi-famous Commodore – he enlisted in the US navy. While serving, he became editor of *The Broadside*, a magazine for Naval Reserve personnel, and his short stories proved a big hit among the servicemen (they would later be reprinted, selling more than 70,000 copies). Five years after being discharged from the Navy in 1919, Thorne gave up his job in advertising – an industry he despised, but which he continually fell back on in order to make money – to devote himself full-time to writing. In 1926, he published the novel that made his name: *Topper: An Improbable Adventure.* A comedy fantasy novel about a respectable banker called Cosmo Topper and his misadventures with a couple of ghosts, Marion and George Kerby, *Topper* was a great success. In 1937, MGM adapted it into a film, with Cary Grant playing George Kerby. Smith eventually wrote a three-book *Topper* series, all of which were adapted into films, as well as a 78 episode television series.

Smith published ten more novels during the rest of his life (including the other two of the *Topper* trilogy), his most ambitious of which was *Dream's End* (1927), a florid, serious Gothic romance featuring heavily symbolic dreams. However, Smith was undoubtedly best known for his humorous works. Indeed, although somewhat neglected now, Smith is regarded by critics as one of the top writers of American comic fiction to come out of the twenties. He died of a heart attack in 1934 while on holiday in Florida, aged just 42.

A Smoky Lady in Knickers

Mr Topper was in an unspeakable frame of mind. He shook himself free from the invisible grasp that had made a retreat of his departure, and fumed up the street, escape his one desire. And every time he passed a drug store a slight tugging at his sleeve informed him that he was not alone, that for him escape was impossible.

"Stop doing things to my sleeve," he growled. "Stop pushing."

"But I want you to buy me a soda," came the whispered reply.

"After all you've done to me you ask me that?" exclaimed the outraged man, for the moment forgetting his fear of being caught talking to himself in the streets. "Fiddling with my hat and stick. Giving my secretary a nervous fit. Why didn't you bawl and scream?"

"But you took such a long time in that horrid old place," the voice pleaded. "And that ridiculous woman looked at you so familiarly. I wanted to pull her ribbons off, but . . ."

"Let me understand this," interrupted Mr Topper, seeking refuge in a nearby doorway. "Am I no longer to dictate to my secretary? Do you object? By what right? I've never compromised you, although God knows you've ruined my reputation – you and your husband. Why don't you torture him and leave me alone?"

"He's left me," the voice replied with just a hint of moisture. "He's gone to sea for a change."

"He needs one," said Mr Topper. "Haven't you any friends?"

"None that I like as well as you. Please don't go on any more. It would be funny to see tears dropping from no place in particular."

The woman was actually hugging him in broad daylight. Mr Topper swayed forward, then with a supreme effort regained both his balance and his composure.

"Don't do that again, ever," he commanded.

"Let's be glad," Marion pleaded. "I didn't mean any harm. George was gone and I didn't have anything to do, so I just went down to the station to see the trains come in and then I saw you and I wanted to

A Smoky Lady in Knickers

go along. It's awfully lonely being a low-planed spirit. You don't know."

Now there had been very little wheedling practised on Mr Topper in the course of his married life. Mrs Topper had arranged everything and Topper had followed the arrangements. On those rare occasions when he had balked Mrs Topper had instantly assumed the rôle of a martyred woman and in pallid silence cherished her indigestion. It was a strange, fearful and fascinating sensation that Mr Topper now experienced as Marion Kerby clung to his neck and asked him to buy her a soda. He forgot the humiliation of the office out of sheer sympathy for the poor, parched spirit who had been the cause of it.

"But hang it, Marion," he said in a softer voice, "be reasonable. How can I buy you a soda?"

"You can pretend to be drinking it," she replied eagerly, "and when you hold your glass aside to look at your newspaper I can sip through the straw. No one will notice it. Just hold your glass a little to one side and I'll come close to you and sip through the straw – little, quiet sips. But you must only pretend to be drinking it. Don't forget yourself."

"I'd rather risk the chance of a scandal and have you materialise," said Mr Topper thoughtfully.

"All right," replied Marion. "I'll do that in a jiffy."

"Not here!" Mr Topper protested. "For once show some restraint. Can't you go somewhere to materialise and then come back to me?"

"How about that shop?" suggested Marion.

The shop she referred to was a small notion shop which owed its existence to the fact that women, regardless of their means, must be clad in silk or near silk against the ever-present dangers of being run over, unexpectedly married or caught in a sudden gale. The shop seemed suitable to Topper for the business of materialisation. He said as much and Marion Kerby departed, declaring that she would be right back in a minute. Mr Topper waited ten before he became impatient, then he walked slowly past the shop and peered through the door. As he did so a hatless woman came bounding forth with stark terror gleaming in her eyes. She was speedily followed by a small boy, who in turn was closely pursued by a man whose features were working frantically. Before Mr Topper could recover from his surprise three girls dashed from the shop and joined their companions in flight, now huddled compactly at a safe distance from the shop. Mr Topper felt like running, too, but curiosity overcame his fear. He approached the group and asked questions. One of the girls looked at him and began to cry.

"Mamma!" she gulped. "Mamma!"

He quickly transferred his gaze to the man.

"What's happened in there?" asked Mr Topper.

"Don't go in, sir," pleaded the man, for the first time in his life discouraging a prospective customer from entering his place of business. "For God's sake, sir, stay here with us."

Topper looked at the boy.

"Little boy," he said, "tell me what frightened all these people."

"I'm not frightened," declared the boy, "but they all started to run and I just got ahead."

"Yes, but why did they start to run?" continued Mr Topper patiently.

"Because of her," said the boy, pointing to the shop.

"Of whom?" demanded Topper.

"The smoky lady who was trying on knickers and everything," answered the boy.

At this point the woman who had been the first to seek comfort in flight found her tongue. A crowd had begun to gather and she addressed herself to the crowd.

"She was all smoky," the woman announced. "And you could see right through her. How I first came to notice her was when I pulled back a curtain to show one of

A Smoky Lady in Knickers

these girls some knickers. There she was, as calm as life, trying on a pair of knickers, a pair of our best knickers, and she was all smoky and transparent so that only the knickers seemed real. When she saw us she got scared and went bounding round the shop so that it looked like a pair of knickers come to life and gone mad. I started to run . . ."

"And I made a grab for the knickers," interrupted the man, "but the smoky woman wouldn't let go, so I just decided that, before any trouble started, I'd run out and see what had happened to Lil."

"It was awful," proclaimed one of the girls. "I'll never forget those knickers dancing round the shop."

"Our best knickers," said the woman.

"A good pair," added the man.

"Perhaps they are not a total loss," Mr Topper suggested. "Why not go back and find out? I'll buy the knickers if this smoky woman hasn't walked off with them."

As attractive as the offer was to the proprietor he seemed reluctant to accept.

"Come on," said Mr Topper. "I'll lead the way."

"But, sir, you don't understand," the man protested earnestly. "Have you ever seen a transparent woman dancing about in a real pair of knickers?"

"That depends on what you mean by transparent," replied Mr Topper judiciously. "Anyway, it's much better than seeing a real woman dancing about in a transparent pair of knickers."

At this remark the young lady who had been sobbing for mamma suddenly giggled and looked archly at Mr Topper. The proprietor seemed unconvinced.

"No, it isn't," he said, with a shake of his head. "Nowadays you can see that at most any good show, but not the other, thank God. It isn't what I call natural entertainment – not for me at any rate."

"And while you're standing here talking," Mr Topper

reminded him, "the smoky lady is probably trying on every blessed thing in your shop."

"Well, I'm not going back to watch her," the proprietor proclaimed to the crowd. "If any of you gents want to see a smoky woman trying on underwear you can step right in, but I don't budge without a cop – two cops," he added as an afterthought.

Mr Topper felt a soft, flimsy article being thrust stealthily into his coat pocket. His hand flew to the spot and shoved the thing out of sight. A gentle pressure on the arm indicated that it was time to depart, and a policeman, pushing through the crowd, strengthened Mr Topper in his belief. He permitted himself to be led away by his invisible guide. After several blocks of silent companionship he could no longer restrain his annoyance.

"Now what the devil do you mean by trying on a pair of those things?" he demanded.

"What a crude question!" Marion murmured.

"Your conduct has given me the privilege to ask it," replied Mr Topper.

"Cosmo," she whispered, leaning heavily against him, "I just love nice things."

"You should leave all that stuff behind you now that you're dead," he answered.

"Even spirits have to be modest," said Marion. "And anyway they frightened me. I was getting along fine until that woman pulled back the curtain. I was pretty nearly completely materialised, but that made me so startled I couldn't finish it."

"That was fortunate, to say the least," replied Mr Topper, "considering the condition you were in."

Topper heard a low laugh.

"You're vile all the way through," said Marion Kerby. "Here's a soda shop. Come on in – chocolate with vanilla ice cream."

Mr Topper felt himself being pulled in the direction of

A Smoky Lady in Knickers

the soda shop. He resisted feebly feeling that he had gone through enough for one day.

"Must you have that soda?" he asked.

"Oh, no," Marion replied in a resigned voice. "I can do without it. I'm used to being miserable. One more disappointment will make no difference. Keep me hanging round your office all morning, then send me in to a place to be scared to death, and after that refuse to buy me a soda. Go on, I like harsh treatment. You remind me of my husband, the low creature."

With the chattering courage of a man being placed in the electric chair, Mr Topper walked into the soda shop and seated himself at the counter.

"Vanilla soda with a chocolate ice," he muttered darkly in the direction of a white-clad individual.

"No! No!" whispered Marion excitedly. "You've got it all wrong. Tell him quick. It's chocolate soda with a vanilla ice."

Mr Topper could feel her fluttering on his lap.

"Be still," he whispered, then smiling ingratiatingly at the clerk he added, "I'm afraid, old man, I got that wrong. I want it the other way 'round."

The clerk looked long at Mr Topper, then walked to the other end of the counter and engaged a colleague in a whispered conversation. From time to time they stopped talking to look back at Mr Topper, whose anxiety was mounting with each look.

Marion Kerby in her eagerness was pinching Topper's hand. He pulled his newspaper from his pocket and hid behind it.

"You and your sodas," he growled. "Why can't you keep quiet?"

"But you had it all wrong," protested Marion. "Look out, here he comes now."

When the attendant had placed the glass on the counter Mr Topper idly reached for it with the air of one too deeply engrossed in the news of the day to be interested in a trivial beverage. Leisurely he placed the glass to his lips, then held it aside.

"The straws," whispered Marion. "Must have straws."

"My God," murmured Mr Topper. "Won't you ever be satisfied?"

He procured two straws, plunged them viciously into the soda, then held the glass behind his paper. The liquid immediately began to descend in the glass. From the rapidity of its descent Mr Topper decided that George Kerby had bought his wife very few sodas during her earthly existence.

"Now dig out the ice cream with the spoon," she whispered. "Pretend to be eating it. I'll nibble it off."

"This is going to be pretty," murmured Mr Topper with as much sarcasm as can be packed into a murmur. "You'll have to do better than nibble. You'll fairly have to snap it off."

The nibbling or snapping operation required the use of both of Mr Topper's hands and forced him to abandon the protection of his paper. With an earnest expression, which was perfectly sincere, he endeavoured to give the impression of a man publicly lusting after ice cream. The spoon flew to his avid mouth, but, just before his lips concealed their prize, the ice cream mysteriously vanished. It must be said in favour of Marion Kerby that she met the demands of the occasion. Not once did she fail to claim her own. Not once was Mr Topper allowed to sample that which he most abhorred. When the ice cream had run its course Mr Topper resumed his paper and waited, with a knowledge bred of experience, for the dregs of the soda to be drawn. He had little time to wait. Hollow, expiring, gurgling sounds loudly proclaimed the welcome ending of the soda. With a sigh of relief Mr Topper was about to return the hateful vessel to the counter when he met the eyes of the clerk peering at him over the top margin of the newspaper. They were cold, worldly eyes, yet curious, and they fixed themselves

A Smoky Lady in Knickers

on Mr Topper like two weary suns regarding a newborn star. A nervous muscular reaction contorted Mr Topper's mouth into a smile.

"Do that again," the clerk said. "Do that trick again without me guessing it and I'll give you this."

He dangled some crumpled bills alluringly in Mr Topper's face.

"I can't," replied Mr Topper. "It's hard enough to drink one of your nauseating concoctions, much less two."

"You didn't drink the first one," said the attendant. "What's your game, anyway? I was watching you all the time. Trying to be funny?"

"Not funny," Mr Topper answered, delicately slipping from his seat. "You're wrong there. That was one of the most serious sodas in my life – one of the worst."

"You're one of those funny guys," said the attendant menacingly. "Come back here and I'll tell you exactly what you are."

But Mr Topper did not wait to be told. He hurried from the store and mingled with the crowd.

"It's awful to be cut off from sodas," breathed Marion Kerby.

"I have no sympathy to waste on you," said Mr Topper.

He was hungry, yet he dared not eat. If she had behaved so excitedly in the presence of a soda, what would she do at the sight of food. Mr Topper shuddered. He was thinking of a plate of soup. No, it would never do. He would have to forego luncheon. This was an overwhelming decision. It left Mr Topper shaken. Never had he missed a meal save when his adenoids had been surreptitiously removed many years before. Mr Topper gazed up at the lean cascades of the Woolworth tower through the tragic eyes of a deflated stomach. There was no fortitude in him. He was the abject slave of a passion he longed but feared to indulge. All his friends were eating luncheon now. He wondered what they were having. Menus danced before his eyes. The 'blue plate' of the day brought savoury odours to his nose. Strangely enough it was in this dismal crisis that Marion Kerby came to his aid.

"Isn't it time for your luncheon?" she suggested.

"Past time," said Mr Topper, "but how can I eat with you with me?"

"Food means nothing to me," she replied. "I can take it or leave it as I choose, but you're different. You must eat."

"I feel that way about it myself," admitted Mr Topper. "For once I think you're right, but, frankly, I'm afraid to enter a public place with you. My nerves can't stand it. Too much has happened."

"Come," she said in a changed voice, taking him forcibly by the arm. "I'm going to see that you get your luncheon. Don't bother at all about me. I'm different now. The city went to my head at first. I'll admit it. Those knickers and the ice cream soda got the best of me. I lost control of myself, but now you don't have to worry. Just a cup of tea – nothing more."

"That ends it," declared Mr Topper. "That's enough. I don't eat. I dare say you fully expect me to crouch under a table and hold a plate of tea while you make strangling noises."

Marion Kerby laughed softly.

"I was only joking about the tea," she said. "Honestly, now, I don't really want it. That's true. I should want it, but I don't. There was only one person I ever knew, not counting myself, who couldn't stand tea, and he was a fine but fanatical drunkard. Graze with the herd and I'll keep quiet."

So Mr Topper had his luncheon. It was a tense luncheon, a suspicious, waiting sort of luncheon, one filled with false starts and empty alarms. In spite of everything it was a good luncheon and Marion Kerby behaved splendidly. Once, when Mr Topper used the

A Smoky Lady in Knickers

pepper too violently, a fit of sneezing came from the opposite chair. The waiter was momentarily startled, but immediately adjusted himself to the situation. He realised, as does everyone who knows anything at all about sneezing, that there are no two sneezes alike and that most anything can be expected of a sneezer. He regarded Mr Topper with the commiseration of one whose sneezes were infrequent and well under control, and departed in stately search of a pie à la mode. Nevertheless, he considered Mr Topper as being not quite the usual customer. He had noticed certain little things. Nothing you could put your finger on, but still a trifle different. For instance, why had the tray containing bread risen to meet Mr Topper's outstretched hand? And why had the salt stand behaved so obligingly? How could one account for a menu tilted in space? And, if that was perfectly natural, why had Mr Topper made such strange fluttering movements with his hands? Deep within himself the waiter sensed that all was not well with his table, but the clatter of plates, the demands of his occupation, and the deep-rooted instinct of all people to deny the existence of the unusual successfully maintained him in his poise of sharply chiselled indifference. The generous size of the tip he washed up in his obsequious hands completely restored his faith in the normal order of things. There had been nothing unusual. Mr Topper was a man who desired to dine. The waiter hoped he would do so more frequently at his table. The waiter was one of those people whose tolerance increases with the size of the tip. For a ten-dollar bill he would have respectfully tidied up after a murder and made excuses for the toughness of the corpse.

Later that afternoon Mr Topper was trying on a cap. He was a diffident man about such things, but on this occasion his heart was in his task. The brownish thing that was making his head ridiculous had vague, temporising lines in it of a nervous blue, but to Mr Topper the cap was lovely. To a man or to a woman he would have said harshly that the cap 'would do,' but to himself he had to admit it was lovely. He admired it hugely. It was a good cap. Mr Topper had no difficulty in convincing the salesman that it was a good cap. With suitable apologies the man agreed that it was a very good cap and that it suited Mr Topper well. Mr Topper found himself admiring the salesman. He knew his business, this man – one of the few salesmen with unimpeachable taste. The cap was practically Topper's. All the salesman had to do was to snatch it from Mr Topper's vainglorious head and wrap it up. Mr Topper was willing. He had never purchased such a cap in his life. With the eager timidity of a virgin he hoped to demolish the record of years. He was brazen about it, yet he was shy almost to the point of tenderness. The cap was in the salesman's hands. Mr Topper was reaching for money. The salesman's free hand was politely waiting for the object of Mr Topper's reaching. Then something happened. A new and different cap appeared in the salesman's outstretched hand. With the instinct of his calling he automatically began to sell the new cap. Then he stopped in confusion and looked helplessly at Mr Topper, who was convulsively clutching a roll of bills. Mr Topper refused to meet the salesman's gaze. Instead he glared at the new cap. It was a terrible cap, an obscene, gloating, desperate cap. Its red checks displayed the brazen indifference of deep depravity. Mr Topper was revolted.

"Take it away," he said. "I don't want it."

At this remark the new cap shook threateningly in the salesman's hand. He tried to give it to Mr Topper, but was unsuccessful. Mr Topper backed away.

"I don't want it," he repeated. "I don't like that cap. Please take it away."

The salesman was deeply moved.

"I'm not trying to sell it to you, sir," he said in a low voice, "but somehow I can't help it."

A Smoky Lady in Knickers

He stood before Mr Topper with a cap in either hand. One cap he held almost lovingly, the other he clung to in spite of himself, like a man with a live coal in a nest of dynamite. His lips trembled slightly. He tried to smile. He was mortally afraid that at any moment Mr Topper would depart with a bad opinion of the shop. He could never permit that to happen. With an effort he turned away, but before he had gone many yards he abruptly swung around and came back at a dog-trot. To Mr Topper he gave the appearance of a man who was being held by the scruff of his neck and the seat of his trousers by someone intent on motivating him from the rear. He stopped suddenly in front of Mr Topper and, in an attitude of supplication, offered him the red checked cap. Mr Topper again refused it.

"I must apologise," the man said rather breathlessly, "but I really think you had better take this cap."

In spite of his irritation Mr Topper regarded the salesman with quick sympathy.

"Why have you changed your mind?" he asked. "I've already told you that I hate that cap. It isn't a nice cap. I don't like it."

The salesman was almost chattering. He shook himself like a dog and glanced quickly over his shoulder. Then he approached Mr Topper.

"I haven't changed my mind," he whispered. "I've lost my mind. It isn't the shop. It's me. I'm mad."

Mr Topper was beginning to feel extremely sorry for the salesman. He wanted to do what he could, but he refused to be bullied into buying a cap he utterly loathed, a cap that went against all his instincts.

"It's too bad about your mind," said Mr Topper, "but I don't want that cap. I won't buy it. And if I do buy it I won't wear it. I'm honest about that."

"Listen," whispered the salesman. "I'll give you the cap if you'll only take it away."

"If you're as anxious as all that to get rid of the

cap," Mr Topper replied, "I'll buy them both. How much are they?"

"Practically nothing," said the salesman, his face clearing. "I'll wrap them up myself."

He hurried away.

"But I won't wear it," said Mr Topper, addressing space. "You won't be able to force the thing on my head."

"Here they are," announced the salesman, returning with the package. "You've been very nice about it, I'm sure."

As the elevator bearing Mr Topper to the ground floor began its descent a low gasp was heard in the car.

"I can't stand these things," whispered Marion Kerby. "They always take my breath."

At each floor the gasp was repeated, whereat Mr Topper cringed under the curious eye of the operator. Mr Topper pretended to gasp in order to protect himself. He smiled sickly at the operator and said:

"Did it affect you that way at first? It always does me."

The operator continued to look at him, but made no answer. He was glad to see the last of Mr Topper. He was afraid that the man was going to swoon in his car.

On the train that evening Mr Topper tried to hide himself in his newspaper, but was unsuccessful. Marion Kerby insisted on turning back the pages and scanning the advertisements. At last Mr Topper abandoned the newspaper and looked out of the window. Presently he became conscious of the fact that several passengers were regarding the vacant seat beside him with undisguised interest. The newspaper was slanted against the air as though it were being held by unseen hands. Mr Topper seized the paper and thrust it into his pocket.

"Rotter!" whispered Marion Kerby.

"Fiend!" muttered Mr Topper.

A heavy personage attempted to occupy the seat,

A Smoky Lady in Knickers

but arose with a grunt of surprise. For a moment he regarded Mr Topper bitterly, but that distraught gentleman was gazing at the landscape with the greedy eyes of a tourist.

At the end of the trip he hurried home. His day had been crammed with desperate events. There would be nothing for him at home save Scollops, but at present Mr Topper preferred a sleepy cat to an active spirit. He yearned for repose.

"Goodbye," said Marion Kerby as he was turning into the driveway. "I've had an awfully nice time and I want to thank you."

"Why did you make me buy that cap?" demanded Mr Topper.

"Because I knew it would look well on you," she answered. "George had one once and everybody liked it."

"Well, I don't, and I won't wear it," said Mr Topper. "Goodbye."

Marion Kerby clung to his arm.

"Don't be angry," she pleaded. "I've got to go back now and it's going to be lonely out there without even George to haggle with. Say goodbye nicely and call me Marion."

Mr Topper had a twinge of conscience. He was going away in the morning without even telling her about it. He was running away from her. Although he realised that he was in no way bound to Marion Kerby, he nevertheless felt guilty in abandoning her, particularly in the absence of her irresponsible husband. However, if he confided in her everything would be ruined. She would be sure to come along. He knew he would never be able to drive her off. After all, why should he not take her along? Then he remembered the events of the day and decided that there was every reason in the world for leaving her behind. He was going away for a rest and not a riot. With Marion Kerby with him rest would be out of the question.

"Well," he said in a mollified voice, "it's not going to be any too crisp for me at home, but I'll look you up in a few days. We'll take a ride together."

"Goodbye," she said, her voice sounding strangely thin and far away. "Don't forget. I'll be waiting for you."

The house had lost none of its funereal atmosphere during Mr Topper's absence. Mrs Topper was sitting in the shadows with her hands folded in her lap. She was the picture of resignation.

"Are you feeling better, my dear?" asked Mr Topper.

"I haven't been thinking about myself," she replied. "There are other things on my mind."

Mr Topper discreetly refrained from asking her what they were. He sat down and read the paper until the maid announced dinner, then he followed his wife into the dining-room, where the evening meal was consumed in silence. He felt like a convict being entertained by a member of a Christian Endeavour Society. Mrs Topper made it a point to see that he was properly served. She seemed to derive a sort of mournful pleasure in watching him chew his food.

When they were once more in the sitting-room Mr Topper announced the fact that he was going away for a trip. It was a difficult announcement to make and Mrs Topper was not helpful. She listened in silence until he was through, then she said without looking at him:

"I hope that for my sake you'll try to keep out of jail."

"It's not a habit," replied Mr Topper. "It was an accident, an unfortunate misunderstanding."

Mrs Topper bent over her sewing and compressed her lips.

"I'll never forget it to my dying day," she said. "The shame and humiliation of it."

"You could forget it if you wanted to," answered Mr Topper. "If you liked me instead of yourself you could forget a lot of things."

A Smoky Lady in Knickers

Mrs Topper regarded her husband with melancholy eyes.

"You ask me to forget that?" she asked.

"Come, Mary," replied Mr Topper in an earnest voice. "I don't know what got into me. I was all wrong, but just the same . . ."

He stopped and, pulling the knickers from his pocket, began to mop his face with them. They were orchid-coloured knickers heightened in attractiveness by crimson butterflies and lace insertion. They gave Mr Topper a foppish appearance. As he stood before his wife with his face nonchalantly buried in the silken fabric Mr Topper looked almost giddy. A new light came into Mrs Topper's eyes. It was the light of despair masking behind outraged modesty. At the height of his mopping Mr Topper must have realised the situation, for he suddenly withdrew his face from its tender concealment and peered at Mrs Topper over the knickers. Mrs Topper had risen. As she confronted her husband she was trembling slightly. He tried to speak, but she held up a restraining hand.

"I refuse to remain in the room and have you flaunt your infidelity in my face," she said. "Don't speak to me. Don't try to explain. Everything is perfectly clear."

"But I bought them for you," gasped Mr Topper. "They were to be a surprise."

"They were a surprise," replied Mrs Topper as she left the room recoiling from the offending garment. "They were a *shock!*"

Printed by Libri Plureos GmbH in Hamburg, Germany